The Three Little Teddy Bears

Book 1

The Little Teddy Bears Series by Lela Belviy

Lela Belviy
9/24/20

The Three Little Teddy Bears by Lela Belviy

Published by Pen It! Publications, LLC in the U.S.A.
812-371-4128 www.penitpublications.com

ISBN: 978-1-952894-46-6

Illustrated by Emily Ann evans

Dedication

This story is dedicated to my niece,
Sheri. I made up this story for her
when she was a little girl.
She loved it and had me tell it to
her over and over.

Once upon a time, there were three little teddy bears.

The teddy bears had been newly made and were ready to be placed in Poppy's Pretty Toy Palace.

One bear was blue, one was pink, and one was a plain beige color.

At the Toy Palace, children would come every day and look for a toy they could love and cherish.

The three teddy bears were so excited – they would soon have a little boy or girl choose them as their forever bear. What a happy day that would be for all three teddy bears.

Poppy carefully placed the blue teddy, the pink teddy, and the plain beige teddy bear on a shelf.
They were now ready for their new owner. When would it happen for each teddy bear?
Every day each teddy bear would comb their fur and brush their teeth. They wanted to look their best.

After only a week, a little boy named Bobby came to the Toy Palace. His parents told him he could choose anything from the Toy Palace.

The three teddy bears that were sitting on the shelf were so excited. They stood up straight and tall and put on their biggest smile.

Bobby looked at the basketballs. He looked at the GI Joes. He looked at the Match Cars. When he saw the blue teddy bear, Bobby KNEW he had found his forever bear.

Poppy reached up and got the blue teddy bear. His parents paid for the bear and Bobby took it home to be loved and cherished forever.

Now just the pink teddy bear and the plain beige teddy bear were left on the shelf. Who would be next?

A couple of weeks went by and one day a little girl named Lula Mae came to the store. She looked at the Barbie dolls. She looked at the baby dolls. She looked at the My Little Ponies. Then she saw the pink teddy bear and she KNEW she had found her forever bear.

Poppy reached up and got the pink teddy bear. Lula Mae's parents paid for the bear and she took it home to be loved and cherished forever.

Lula Mae was so happy.

Now just the plain beige teddy bear was left. When would his special boy or girl come to choose him? He was so excited! He wanted to be someone's forever bear so he could love and be loved.

Every day the plain beige teddy bear would comb his fur and brush his teeth. He wanted to look perfect for his special boy or girl. But no matter how he tried to look good, he knew he was still just a plain beige teddy bear. He often would wonder to himself, just what little girl or boy could love a plain beige teddy bear like him.

Weeks went by and no one bought the plain beige teddy bear.

Months went by and years went by and no one even looked at the plain beige teddy bear anymore.

He was starting to get dusty and he was looking quite old.

The plain beige teddy bear was so sad. Even though he was just an old plain beige teddy bear, he was full of love. All he wanted to do was share that love with someone.

Now it just so happened there was a beautiful little blond-headed girl named Sheri that lived in the block next to Poppy's Pretty Toy Palace.

Her family was very poor and there usually wasn't enough money for Sheri to buy toys.

One day her
parents gave her
ten pennies to
spend however
she wanted.

Sheri had never seen that much money before and she couldn't believe she was going to be able to buy something at the Toy Palace.

She walked by Poppy's Pretty Toy Palace every day and would longingly look through the windows.

Today she was going to walk in that store and actually buy something. It was the happiest day of her life.

She walked up and down the aisles of the Toy Palace. There were so many toys; she didn't know what to do. Then it happened!

She saw the plain beige teddy bear sitting up on that shelf. She felt the teddy bear was perfect, so Sheri asked Poppy how much the teddy bear cost.

He lovingly reached up and got the teddy bear off the shelf.
At that moment, Sheri realized that ten pennies just wasn't very much money.

Poppy noticed a tear streaming down Sheri's face.
That made Poppy so sad.

Poppy looked at the price tag on the bear, and then looked at Sheri and he said.

"Sheri, 10 pennies is exactly how much this plain beige bear costs."

Sheri got the biggest smile on her face and Poppy placed the teddy bear in Sheri's arms.

She gave her forever bear the
GREATEST hug ever.

Then do you know what happened?
Love filled the plain beige teddy
bear from the top of his ears to the
tips of his toes.

Poppy couldn't believe it.
The teddy bear was simply glowing
all over. The plain beige teddy bear
had become the most handsome
teddy bear he had ever seen
in his life.

Sheri and her new teddy bear
named Sugarboo Bear went home
to cherish and love each other
FOREVER.

Isn't it amazing what love can do,
if given a chance?

The End

Author Lela Belviy was born in the small town of St. Francisville, Illinois. She has lived in Indiana since 1982, living in Indianapolis for 25 years, and then she moved to Seymour, Indiana. Lela was a foster parent for 10 years and was fortunate and blessed enough to adopt two of her children. She strongly believes in the power of God and loves seeking God's path for her life. Lela is married to her wonderful husband, Bob. Together, they have three girls and have been blessed with six adorable grandchildren.

Ms. Belviy worked for a major insurance company for a total of 40 years and retired in 2017. She has always made up stories for her nieces, nephews, children, and grandchildren. They loved the stories and would often ask her to tell them again and again. Unfortunately, she didn't always remember exactly how she told the story the first time. Eventually, Lela decided to start writing those stories down. Recently her family and friends encouraged her to try to publish them, so she reached out to Pen It! Publications and together they were blessed to be able to bring her stories to life. It is her hope you enjoy the stories as much as she enjoyed writing them.